THE CASE OF THE
DiAMONds iN THE DESK

by Lewis B. Montgomery
illustrated by Amy Wummer

The KANE PRESS
New York

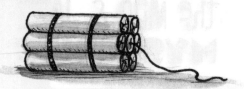

Text copyright © 2012 by Lewis B. Montgomery
Illustrations copyright © 2012 by Amy Wummer
Super Sleuthing Strategies original illustrations copyright © 2012 by Kane Press, Inc.
Super Sleuthing Strategies original illustrations by Nadia DiMattia

Library of Congress Cataloging-in-Publication Data

Montgomery, Lewis B.
The case of the diamonds in the desk / by Lewis B. Montgomery ; illustrated by Amy
Wummer.
p. cm. -- (The Milo & Jazz mysteries ; 8)
Summary: Detectives-in-training Milo and Jazz must work backward to solve the
case of the diamonds that mysteriously appeared in Milo's desk at school.
ISBN 978-1-57565-391-4 (pbk.) -- ISBN 978-1-57565-392-1 (library binding) --
ISBN 978-1-57565-393-8 (e-book)
[1. Mystery and detective stories. 2. Schools--Fiction.] I. Wummer, Amy, ill. II. Title.
PZ7.M7682Cagm 2012
[Fic]--dc23
2011040121

1 3 5 7 9 10 8 6 4 2

First published in the United States of America in 2012 by Kane Press, Inc.
Printed in the United States of America
WOZ0112

Book Design: Edward Miller

The Milo & Jazz Mysteries is a registered trademark of Kane Press, Inc.

Visit us online at **www.kanepress.com**

 Like us on Facebook
facebook.com/kanepress

 Follow us on Twitter
@kanepress

For the Setliffs, naturally!
—L.B.M.

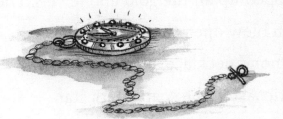

CHAPTER ONE

Milo slouched at his desk, gazing at the board without really seeing it. He was thinking about stolen jewels.

Ever since he'd seen the news report the night before, he couldn't get it off his mind. A real jewel heist! Just like in *Whodunnit* magazine!

The thieves had broken into a big jewelry store in the middle of the night. They smashed the glass showcases and scooped up all the gold and jewels. They even blew open the vault and stole a diamond necklace and tiara made for Trixie Astor, the soap opera star.

Police were baffled. The jeweler's insurance company was offering a $1 million reward.

Milo smiled dreamily. If only he and Jazz had a case like *that* to solve!

Milo and his friend Jazz were detectives in training. They got lessons in the mail from world-famous sleuth Dash Marlowe.

Together, Milo and Jazz had solved a bunch of cases right there in the town of Westview. But never anything like this. He could see the flashbulbs popping as they stepped forward for their reward.

Maybe Dash Marlowe would show up!
Dash would shake their hands and say—
"Milo, how many muffins do I have?"
Mr. Davenport asked.

"Huh?" Milo stared at his teacher. Behind him, a girl giggled.

Mr. Davenport tapped his marker on the board. "I baked a batch of two dozen muffins. I ate a quarter of them. Then I baked two more batches and ate a third. So now what do I have?"

Milo struggled to think, then gave up. Weakly, he said, "A stomach ache?"

The teacher sighed. "Anyone else?"

As hands shot up around the room, Noah and Carlos twisted in their seats to give Milo

sympathetic looks. He was glad the two of them were in his class this year, especially with Jazz banished across the hall. He missed all those notes written in invisible ink.

After math was art. As the students pulled their art smocks from their desks, Mr. Davenport called Milo up.

"Something special on your mind today?" the teacher asked.

Milo swallowed. "Well, uh . . ."

"Listen, I know right now math may not seem—" Mr. Davenport broke off, his head whipping around. "Well, for the love of Pete!"

Mr. Davenport dashed to the window and stared out. Milo followed him. All he saw was the empty playground.

"I could have sworn . . ." The teacher
shook his head and turned back to Milo.
"So, ah . . . I was saying . . ." He frowned.
"What was I saying?"

"Um . . . math?" Milo said.

"Math. Yes. Right." Mr. Davenport glanced out the window again. "Well . . . try to keep your head in the game from now on, okay?"

"I will," Milo promised.

To his relief, the teacher let him go. The other students had already lined up at the door.

Milo ran to his desk. He pulled the top open, grabbed his folded smock—and froze.

Something glittered in his desk. Something like . . . diamonds.

CHAPTER TWO

Diamonds?

Slowly, Milo reached into his desk. He
felt the cool, hard stones under his fingers
as he picked up the object. It really was!
A diamond necklace! In his desk!

"Care to join us, Milo?"

Startled, he dropped the necklace back
into the desk and slammed it shut. Mr.
Davenport watched from the door as
Milo rushed to join his classmates, who
were filing out into the hall.

His mind was in a whirl. Where had the necklace come from? And how did it get in his desk? Could this be connected to the jewel heist he'd seen on TV?

In the art room, he tried to focus on  his toothpick sculpture, but it was impossible. Finally, while the art teacher was helping another student, Milo slipped out of the room. He had to look at that necklace again!

He hurried down the hall, hoping that Mr. Davenport was taking a break in the teachers' lounge. But when he walked in, his teacher was crouched by Milo's desk, staring down at the floor.

What was he doing? Milo wondered.

Oh, no! What if Mr. Davenport had looked *inside* the desk? What if he'd seen the necklace?

Mr. Davenport jumped up. "What are you doing here?"

"I, uh . . ." Milo scrambled for an excuse. "I felt funny in art class. I think the glue smell made me woozy."

His teacher gave him an odd look. "Do you need to go to the nurse?"

Milo shook his head. What did that look mean? Maybe Mr. Davenport had seen the news of the jewel heist, too. Maybe he thought Milo was the thief. Maybe he'd already called the police!

Mr. Davenport checked the clock. "Art class is almost over. Why don't you sit down and rest?"

Milo sat and stared at his closed desk. He didn't dare open it with his teacher in the room. If only he had X-ray vision!

Math homework
p. 122-125

At last, Mr. Davenport left to pick up the rest of the class from art. The instant he stepped out the door, Milo flipped up the lid. The necklace was still there, untouched.

Quickly, he slid it out and tucked it in the pocket of his jeans. He had to show it to Jazz. She would help figure out what to do.

It seemed like hours before the bell rang for recess. As the students piled out the door, Noah asked Milo, "Want to play foursquare?"

"I can't today."

Carlos came up on Milo's other side. "You have to! If you don't, Spencer will want Mandy to play."

"What's wrong with Mandy?" Milo asked. Mandy was a terrific ball player, maybe the best in their whole grade.

His friends gave each other a look.

"It isn't Mandy," Noah explained. "It's Spencer. He's awful around her."

Carlos made kissy noises.

"*Oh.*" Milo hated to let them down, but he couldn't think about foursquare at a time like this. He had to talk to Jazz.

He found her hanging on the zip line. When she saw him she dropped down, brushing her hands. He grabbed her arm and dragged her toward the far end of the playground.

"Hey, what are you— Milo! Quit pulling!"

18

Letting go, Milo glanced around to make sure nobody was watching. Then he pulled the diamond necklace from his pocket. Cupping it in his hands, he gave her a quick peek.

Jazz's eyes widened. "Wow! Where did that come from?"

"I found it in my desk."

"Your *desk*? How did it get in there?"

"I don't know," he said. "I went to get my art smock out and—there it was!"

"You mean it wasn't there when you came in?" Jazz asked.

Milo tried to think. This morning, just like always, he had unloaded his backpack and dumped his books and homework into his desk. He certainly hadn't seen the diamond necklace then.

But had he even looked?

"I'm not sure," he admitted.

Jazz took the necklace and held it up.
The diamonds sparkled in the sunlight.
"Do you think they're real?"

Milo snatched the necklace back and stuffed it in his pocket. "Sure they are. Those thieves know what they're doing."

"Thieves? What thieves?" Jazz asked.

As Milo told her about the jewel heist, she lifted an eyebrow.

"But that store is in the city," she said. "It's hours away. What would the jewels be doing here?"

"Maybe the thieves are hiding out," he said.

"In Westview? Why?"

"Why not? Nobody would expect to find them here."

Jazz frowned. "Well, when we turn the necklace in—"

"Turn it in? But it's a clue!"

She stared at him. "Milo, you're not

thinking about trying to solve this case?"

"Sure!" he said. "Why not? We've solved plenty of others."

"But if these are actually stolen diamonds, this is serious. A real crime."

"That's why it's our big chance!"

Jazz shook her head. "I think we should tell someone."

"We will," he promised. "Just not right away."

"By the end of the day," Jazz said.

"That's not long enough! A week!"

She looked at him for a long moment. Then she said, "Twenty-four hours. *Tops*. Then, no matter what, we're telling somebody. A teacher. Or our parents. Maybe even the police."

CHAPTER THREE

Milo couldn't wait to get started.

"What should we do first?" he asked.
"Stake out my classroom? Wait! What
about fingerprints?" Pulling the necklace
out again, he peered at it. "I bet there are
fingerprints all over this thing."

"Yeah," Jazz said. "Yours and mine."

Oops.

"Well, the thieves probably wore
gloves, anyway," he said.

Jazz frowned. "You know, we can't be sure that these are stolen diamonds. Maybe one of the girls in your class brought them to school."

"How many girls our age have diamond necklaces?" Milo asked. "And even if one of the girls *did* have one, why would she wear it to school?"

"The diamonds could be fake."

"They don't look fake to me," he said.

"Well . . . me neither." Jazz shrugged. "But we're not experts. Anyway, we should at least find out if anybody lost a necklace."

Milo had to admit that made sense. They divvied up the girls—five for him, six for her—and headed off in opposite directions.

Jazz was the first one back. As Milo jogged up, she told him, "No luck here. The closest thing was Brooke—she lost a horse charm off her bracelet. You?"

He shook his head. "And I asked everyone—well, except Mandy. She was playing foursquare and she elbowed me out of the way."

Jazz laughed. "I've never seen Mandy wear jewelry, anyway."

Just then the bell rang for the end of recess. Milo and Jazz agreed to meet in the school library at the end of the day.

When Milo arrived, Jazz wasn't there. He found a free computer and pulled up the latest news about the heist.

"These robbers are real pros," a police spokesperson said. "They studied how the jewelry store operated. They disabled the alarms and broke the cameras. And only somebody who really knew explosives could have blown that vault without sending the whole store sky-high."

As he was reading, Jazz rushed in. "Sorry I'm late! I stopped to see my old kindergarten teacher."

"Huh? What for?"

"Well, I was thinking," she said. "Kindergartners have all that fancy dress-up stuff. . . ."

Milo jumped up. "You didn't tell her what I found!"

Jazz shook her head. "I said I needed a fake diamond necklace for a costume. But she was sure she hadn't put anything like that in the dress-up box."

Milo felt the necklace in his pocket. "I still say it's the real thing."

"We could take it to a jewelry store," Jazz suggested. "They could tell."

"What if it's worth a zillion dollars? They'll ask where we got it. They might even think *we're* the thieves."

Jazz bit her lip. "Well, maybe we could look online. I bet there's a way to tell real diamonds from fake ones."

She reached toward the keyboard, and Milo moved over. Just then, a movement outside the window caught his eye.

"What in the world is he doing?"

"Who?" Jazz asked.

"My teacher." Milo pointed. "I just saw him duck behind that tree. I think he's hiding!"

"*Hiding?*" Jazz repeated. "Why would he do that?"

"I don't know, but I want to find out!"

Not waiting to see if Jazz would

follow, Milo dashed out of the library and down the hall.

Jazz caught up with him as he burst through the exit. Before she could speak, Milo yanked her behind a shrub.

At that moment, a black van swung into the parking lot. Mr. Davenport stepped out from behind the tree.

Jazz poked Milo. "Why are we—"

"Shhh!" he hissed.

Milo peeked around the bush. His teacher was waving with both hands. Not waving exactly—snatching wildly at the air.

A secret signal?

The black van pulled up. A man leaned out and called. "Dynamite Dan!"

Mr. Davenport dropped his arms and

walked toward the van. "Come on, Nick. Nobody calls me that these days. It's ancient history."

The man laughed. "Didn't look so ancient Sunday night. Come on, hop in."

As the van roared off, Jazz stood up. "Want to tell me why we're spying on your teacher?" She waited. "Milo? *Milo?*"

He looked up at her. Slowly he said, "Sunday night."

"What about it?" Jazz demanded.

"Sunday night was when the jewelry store was robbed."

CHAPTER FOUR

"I can't believe you think your teacher is a jewel thief!" Jazz said again.

"You keep saying that," Milo said.

"Well, I can't!"

They had been arguing the whole way home. The less Jazz listened to him, the more certain Milo became.

"He's been acting weird all day. This morning he went running to the window, but when I looked out, there was nothing there. Then, later, I saw him crouching

on the floor next to my desk. And now—
hiding behind a tree!"

"Grownups always act funny," Jazz
said. "My dad dances to the music in the
supermarket."

"But what about what we just heard? *Sunday night*."

"Milo, that makes no sense at all. Everybody did *something* Sunday night," Jazz said.

"Something to do with being called Dynamite Dan?" he pressed. "One of the robbers was an expert with explosives."

Jazz didn't answer right away. Then she said, "Suppose Mr. Davenport really is a jewel thief. Wouldn't he want to keep the diamonds? Why would he put them in your desk?"

"Maybe somebody was coming, and he had to hide them quick. Or maybe—" Milo gulped. "Do you think he wanted to frame me?"

"Milo, he's your *teacher*!"

"That could be a cover. You know, Mr. Davenport is new this year. How do we know he's really a teacher at all?"

Jazz groaned. "Well, you can worry about phony teachers. *I'm* going to find out about phony diamonds."

They dropped their backpacks in Milo's front hall and headed straight to the computer. While Milo looked over her shoulder, Jazz typed in "diamond real or fake." She clicked on the first result.

"It says here that a real diamond can scratch glass. That's the most famous way to tell a real diamond from a fake."

Pulling the necklace from his pocket, Milo glanced around the room. "There's the window—"

"Milo! Your mom would kill you!"

Jazz said. "Anyway, it says that isn't a good test. Some fake diamonds can scratch glass too."

"So how are we supposed to tell?"

Jazz scrolled down. "We could try the fog test."

"What's that?" Milo asked.

"You breathe on it. If the diamond gets foggy, like a mirror, it's a fake. But if it's clear, it's real."

They bent their heads together over the necklace. Milo took a deep breath in, then let it out. *Huuuuuuuunnhhh* . . .

Jazz reeled back. "Your breath smells terrible! What did you have for lunch?"

"Jazz, look!"

The diamonds were sparkling clear.

Milo and Jazz stared at each other.

"They are real!" Milo said.

"Sure looks that way," Jazz agreed. "Wow!"

Just then, they heard a key turning in the front door. Quickly, Milo shoved the necklace in his pocket.

His mom came in lugging a load of groceries, her keys in one hand and the day's mail in the other. His little brother, Ethan, trailed behind, making Darth Vader noises through his nose.

"Something for you," his mom said, dropping an envelope by the computer.

A new lesson from Dash Marlowe!

Jazz hung over Milo's shoulder as he tore open the envelope.

DASH MARLOWE

SECRETS OF A SUPER SLEUTH!

Work Backward

"Begin at the beginning," people always say. But for a sleuth, that isn't always good advice. To solve a case, often you have to begin at the end—then work backward to the beginning.

Once, I worked backward to solve an unusual theft at an amusement park. A teenage girl was waiting in the roller coaster line, when suddenly her purse was snatched away—by a big brown dog!

She chased the dog, but it disappeared into the crowd. The alarm was raised, and a few minutes later the amusement park staff nabbed the dog as it splashed happily at the bottom of the river rapids ride. But the purse was gone.

Luckily, I happened to be on the scene. I asked the people in line which way the dog had come from, and they pointed to the house of mirrors. From there, I traced the dog's path back to the merry-go-round, the swinging pirate ship, and the Tilt-a-Whirl. Everyone had seen the big brown dog, but nobody had seen the purse.

Then I asked a little boy who had just gotten off the Tilt-a-Whirl. He told me the dog had come from the snack stand with a slice of pizza hanging from its mouth. "I'm hungry," the boy added.

I questioned the young man who ran the snack stand. He immediately pulled the missing purse out from behind the counter. When he'd seen the dog running by with it, he'd held out a slice of pizza and the dog had dropped the purse. The young man explained that he was planning to turn in the purse as soon as his shift ended.

The girl was happy to get her purse back. She rewarded the little boy with a slice of pizza and said he was super cute. She said the dog was super cute, too. And the young man at the snack stand . . . well, the last I saw, he was helping the girl into a boat for two at the Tunnel of Love.

"So we need to work backward," Milo said. "That means we should try to figure out everywhere Mr. Davenport has been since Sunday night."

Jazz shook her head.

"But Dash says—"

"I don't think it's Mr. Davenport's movements we need to trace," she said. "I think it's the necklace."

"How are we supposed to do that?" Milo asked. "It's not like my classroom has security cameras or anything."

Jazz didn't answer. Then, suddenly,

she hopped off her stool and grabbed her jacket.

"Where are you going?" he asked.

"Back to school."

"But everybody's gone."

"Not everybody," Jazz replied. "Somebody is still there. And I think that somebody might be able to tell us how the diamonds got into your desk."

CHAPTER FIVE

The doors to the school were locked. Milo pressed his face to the glass. Inside, the hall was shadowy and dim.

Jazz tugged at his sleeve. "Come on!"

He followed her around the building. She peered in each classroom window as she passed. Stopping at one, she rapped it with her knuckles.

"Mrs. Peach!" She rapped again, more loudly. "MRS. PEACH!"

The door to the playground opened.

Mop in hand, the custodian leaned out. "Hey, kids. What's up?"

Jazz stepped forward. "Mrs. Peach, did you find a lost necklace yesterday? Fancy? It looked like diamonds?"

"Necklace." The custodian frowned. Then her face cleared. "Oh, sure, yeah. Stuck it in the desk."

Jazz shot Milo a triumphant look.

"*You* put that necklace in my desk?" He stared at Mrs. Peach.

"Yours, huh?" She shook her mop at him. "You kids. If you didn't have so much stuff, maybe you'd learn to take better care of it."

"But—but it's not my—"

Jazz broke in. "Do you remember where you found the necklace?"

"Right there on the floor by the desk," Mrs. Peach said. "That's why I put it in. Otherwise, it'd go to Lost and Found."

Milo said, "You didn't think that was kind of a funny thing to find in school? A diamond necklace?"

Mrs. Peach looked at him. "Honey, you would not believe the things I find. An empty bottle labeled 'Liquid Butt'?"

Jazz wrinkled her nose. "That was one of Gordy Fletcher's pranks. It smells like—"

"I *know*," Mrs. Peach said. "Anyway, I figured the diamonds had to be fake. Who'd bring a real diamond necklace to school?"

Milo shot Jazz a sideways glance. That was the question. Who *would* bring diamonds to school? And why?

The custodian told them she needed to get back to work. As the door closed behind her, Jazz said, "Now we know how the necklace got in your desk."

"But how did it get on the floor?" Milo asked.

"Whoever had it must have dropped it by mistake," Jazz said.

"Mr. Davenport."

"Or somebody else."

"Like who?" Milo said. "One of the boys in my class? We already asked all the girls."

"Except for Mandy."

They looked at each other.

"We have to hurry," Milo said. "Dad promised to bring Chinese takeout home, and Ethan is an egg roll fiend." If Milo wasn't there, his little brother wouldn't leave him anything but drippy broccoli.

Mandy's house was only two blocks from the school. They found her outside, bouncing a soccer ball from knee to knee. When she saw them, she grinned. "Think fast!"

Whoomph. The ball smacked into Milo's stomach.

As he doubled over, Mandy said,

"Oh . . . sorry. You okay?"

Jazz scooped the ball from the ground and tossed it to Mandy. The other girl trapped it with her foot and flipped it back up to her knees.

"Milo found a necklace at school," Jazz said. "Did you lose one?"

"Me?" Mandy shook her head.

Jazz sighed. "Oh, well. I couldn't really picture you in diamonds."

The soccer ball dropped to the ground and rolled away.

"Diamonds," Mandy said slowly. "Can I see them?"

Jazz turned to Milo. He shrugged. Pulling the necklace from his pocket, he dangled it on his fingers.

"Oh, yeah. That's it!" Mandy said.

"That's what?" Jazz asked.

"I did lose it," Mandy explained. "When he gave it to me, I was playing freeze tag. I stuck it in my jacket pocket and forgot about it." She shook her head. "I wish he wouldn't do stuff like that. It's embarrassing."

Milo and Jazz looked at each other.

"Who?" Jazz asked.

A pink flush spread across Mandy's cheeks. "Spencer."

CHAPTER SIX

"Let me get this straight," Jazz said. "Spencer gave you a diamond necklace and you *forgot*?"

"Well, Noah tagged me and unfroze me, so I had to run," Mandy explained. "Besides, it's not like they're *real* diamonds, right? We're talking about Spencer, not Richie Rich."

Milo looked at the stones glittering in his hand. But they *were* real. Where had Spencer gotten them?

Glancing at Jazz, he could tell she was wondering the same thing.

"Can we keep it?" she asked Mandy. "Just until tomorrow?"

Mandy shrugged. "Keep it forever if you like."

Mandy's father called her in to set the table, so they said goodbye and left.

"Okay," Jazz said. "You found the necklace in your desk today, which Mrs. Peach found on the floor last night—"

"Which must have fallen out of Mandy's pocket when she put her jacket on at the end of the day," Milo put in.

"Which Mandy got from Spencer during recess yesterday," Jazz finished. "But where did Spencer get it?" She stopped and pulled out her detective

notebook and her purple sparkle pen.
Then, working backward, she wrote
down each person who'd had the
diamond necklace at school.

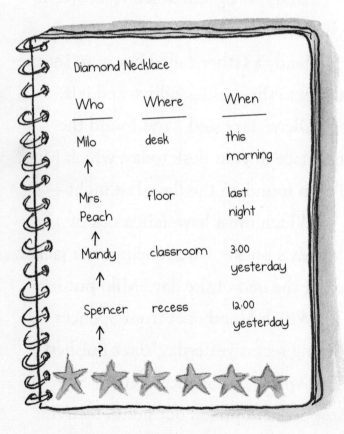

Diamond Necklace

Who	Where	When
Milo ↑	desk	this morning
Mrs. Peach ↑	floor	last night
Mandy ↑	classroom	3:00 yesterday
Spencer ↑ ?	recess	12:00 yesterday

Jazz tapped her pen against her teeth. "So now the question is: who did Spencer get the necklace from?"

"Mr. Davenport? Dynamite Dan?"

"Milo!"

"Well, Spencer didn't *buy* a diamond necklace, that's for sure. Mandy is right. He isn't a boy millionaire."

Milo thought about their friend. Spencer tended to get a bit carried away. Giving Mandy an over-the-top present was just his style.

But would he steal to do it? That, Milo couldn't believe. Nobody he knew was more honest than Spencer.

So how did he get the necklace?

Jazz looked worried, too. "We need to talk to Spencer."

"I'll call him right after dinner."

She shook her head. "I think we should go to his house. Now."

Milo could almost smell the wontons disappearing down his brother's throat. Did Dash Marlowe ever have to make a sacrifice like this to solve a case?

He sighed. "Okay, let's go."

Spencer answered the door with his parrot, Floyd, perched on his shoulder. "Hey, guys! Come in!"

Milo edged inside, keeping clear of Floyd's sharp beak. That parrot had it in for him.

"RELAX!" Floyd screeched.

Milo jumped back.

Spencer laughed. "My mom's got a new meditation CD she plays when I'm at school. It's supposed to make her feel peaceful or something. Now Floyd is always telling me to close my eyes and breathe."

"Why can't you breathe with your eyes open?" Milo asked.

Spencer shrugged. "Ask Floyd."

Milo eyed the parrot doubtfully. Floyd glared back at him and snarled, "YOU FEEL CALM AND SAFE."

Jazz said, "Spencer, we were just at Mandy's house and she said you gave her a necklace yesterday."

"Does she like it?" Spencer asked eagerly.

Milo and Jazz exchanged a glance.

Instead of answering, Jazz asked, "Where did you get it?"

Spencer's face changed. He stepped backward. "Uh . . ."

"LET GO," Floyd squawked from his shoulder perch. "FEEL YOUR BODY MELT INTO THE FLOOR."

Spencer looked as if he would be

more than happy to melt into the floor.

"Tell us where you got the necklace," Jazz said. "It's important. Please."

"Okay!" Spencer burst out. "I know I should have taken it to Lost and Found. But it was just lying on the playground. Finders keepers, right?"

"A diamond necklace?" Jazz said.

"Well, I knew it had to be a fake," Spencer explained. "But it was pretty. And Mandy—she's—she's so—"

"Never mind about Mandy," Milo cut in hastily. "Where on the playground?"

Spencer looked surprised. "In the grass near the foursquare court. Why—do you know who lost it?"

"Not yet," Jazz told him. "But we're going to find out."

CHAPTER SEVEN

To Milo's relief, when he got home his parents had just started to unpack the Chinese takeout. Sliding into his place at the table, he dug in.

He was chasing a piece of chicken around the plate with his chopsticks when his father asked, "Did you hear about the robbery on Highland Drive?"

Milo looked up.

"Really, a robbery?" his mother said. "Here?"

His father nodded. "I heard Chief Smalley talking about it at the barber shop. No sign of a break-in, but the woman reported a diamond necklace missing."

 Milo's chopsticks skidded. The chunk of chicken flew across the table, landing in his brother's drink.

Ethan let out a wail. "Ewwww!"

"It was an accident!" Milo said. "Besides, it all ends up in the same place."

"Then *you* drink chicken soda!"

Milo turned to his mother. "Can I please clear my place?"

"I got almond cookies for dessert," his father said.

Milo hesitated. He loved almond cookies. But he had a case to solve.

Cookie . . . or case?

He sighed. "That's okay. I'm full."

Grabbing the phone, he rushed to his room and dialed. Jazz's oldest brother, Dylan, answered. "She's right here."

"Hello?" Jazz said.

Quickly, Milo told her about the robbery on Highland Drive. "You see? This proves it!"

"Proves what?" she asked.

"The jewel thieves really are hiding out here in our town!"

Jazz was silent for a moment. "Milo. You found a diamond necklace, right?"

"Right."

"And the police say that a woman lost a diamond necklace."

"Stolen," he said. "From her house."

"So if it's the same necklace—"

"Got to be!"

"Then how can it have anything to do with the big jewel heist?" Jazz asked.

Oh.

"Okay, maybe our necklace isn't the one they blew the safe for," he admitted. "But the robbers are the same."

"How do you know?"

"Dynamite Dan! I mean, come on. How many explosive experts do we have in Westview?"

"They blew up the woman's house?" Jazz asked.

"Well . . . no. Actually, my dad said there was no sign of a break-in. But that just goes to show what pros they are."

Silence.

"Jazz?"

"We need to go to the police."

"But we're so close!" Milo protested. "And you gave us twenty-four hours to crack the case."

"Milo, we could get in real trouble!" Jazz said.

"I'm the one who has the necklace," he said stubbornly.

Jazz sighed. "I hope jail food tastes better than school lunches. . . . Okay, what do we do next?"

"We need a witness. Somebody who saw Mr. Davenport drop the necklace on the playground."

"If somebody saw him drop it, wouldn't they have told him?" Jazz said. "Anyway, maybe it was someone else."

"Like who? We asked all the girls. You think it was a boy?"

"Or it could have been there before we came out for recess," she pointed out. "The second graders get the playground before us."

"A second grader with a diamond necklace?" Milo said.

"Well, I still think we need to go to the police," Jazz said. "When we give them the necklace, you can tell them your suspicions about Mr. Davenport."

"They'd never believe me," he said. "They'd just say I was mad because he gives us too much homework or something. We need proof."

"Like what?"

He shook his head. "I don't know."

But later in the evening, it came to him. If his teacher had brought one piece of stolen jewelry to school, he could have brought others.

Maybe Mr. Davenport's desk drawers were stuffed with gold and diamonds!

Milo ran to the phone and left a message for Jazz.

"Meet me at school early tomorrow," he said. "I've got a plan."

CHAPTER EIGHT

When Milo arrived at school the next morning, Jazz was waiting outside.

"So, what's your plan?" she asked.

"I'm going to sneak into my classroom and search Mr. Davenport's desk," he said.

Jazz stared at him. "That's not a plan. That's just a really, really bad idea. You can't go digging in a teacher's desk."

"You can if he's a jewel thief."

"Oh, Milo. What if you get caught?" she asked.

"Don't worry. We'll be careful."

"*We?*"

"You only have to be my lookout," Milo explained.

"No!" Jazz crossed her arms and planted her purple clogs firmly on the pavement. "No way!"

Milo knew he didn't have much time. If Mr. Davenport wasn't already in the classroom, he'd be there soon.

"Fine," he said. "I'll do it by myself."
Before Jazz could say anything else, he
pushed into the school.

Inside, he told the monitor he needed
to go to the bathroom, and she nodded.
As soon as she turned away, he headed
the other way down the hall.

The light was on in his classroom.
Milo peeked through the open door.
Nobody there.

Cautiously, he slipped into the room.
He edged toward Mr. Davenport's desk.
All he needed was a minute to check the
drawers and—

"GOTCHA!"

Milo leapt back as Mr. Davenport
dove out headfirst from behind his desk.
The teacher's hand slammed to the floor,

missing Milo's shoe by an inch.

Milo gaped down at him in horror.

Keeping his cupped hand on the floor, Mr. Davenport looked up. *"Murgantia histrionica!"*

The words sounded to Milo like a wizard's spell. He backed away.

"Come here," his teacher ordered.

Reluctantly, Milo moved closer.

Mr. Davenport lifted his hand slowly from the floor. "Look!"

Milo looked. It was . . .

"A *bug*?"

"Murgantia histrionica," the teacher repeated triumphantly. "Harlequin bug. Cute, huh?" He beamed at the tiny red-and-black insect as if it were a puppy.

Milo wasn't sure what to do.

Squatting down, he reached out
cautiously.

Mr. Davenport said, "Oh, I wouldn't
touch—"

Milo yanked his hand away and fell back, spluttering. "It stinks!"

"Oh, yes," Mr. Davenport agreed cheerfully. "One of the stinkbug family. Better go wash your hand."

Milo rushed to the boys' bathroom. As he pumped soap into his palms and scrubbed, he tried to make sense of what had just happened.

Was Mr. Davenport the strangest jewel thief ever? Or did his odd behavior have nothing to do with the heist at all?

Rushing to the window during class to stare at nothing, crawling around on the floor, creeping around outdoors, and grabbing at the air—could it all be about *bugs*?

By the time Milo got back to the

classroom, a faint aroma hovering around him, the rest of the students had come in.

All morning, Milo felt ready to burst.

He had to talk to Jazz!

Finally, the bell rang for recess. Milo rushed out to the playground. As soon as he saw Jazz, the whole story spilled out.

"And I never got to look in his desk," Milo lamented. "Maybe after school—"

"*No,*" Jazz said. "Your twenty-four hours are up. We're going to turn that necklace in. Right now."

CHAPTER NINE

The office lady told Milo and Jazz that they would have to wait to see the principal. They sat down in the chairs.

Near them, a younger girl waited too, slumped miserably in her seat.

"What did you get in trouble for?" Milo asked.

The girl seemed ready to cry. "Nothing! I'm sick!"

"Oh. Sorry."

A worried-looking woman in a business suit rushed in. "Ashley! Honey, are you all right?"

The girl smiled wanly. "Hi, Mom."

"I came as soon as the nurse called!" The woman turned to the office lady. "My boss will have a fit. Yesterday I was late to work because I had to call the police, and now this. . . ."

Police?

"Excuse me," Milo broke in eagerly. "Did you lose a diamond necklace?"

"Why . . . yes, I did," the woman said, looking surprised.

He stood and pulled the necklace from his pocket. "Is this it?"

The woman gasped. "My necklace! But . . . how in the world . . ."

Her daughter burst into tears.

Milo glanced at Jazz. She was staring at the girl.

"What grade are you in?" Jazz asked.

"S-second," she sobbed.

Jazz turned to Milo. "Told you so!"

The girl and her mother gaped at Jazz. But Milo got it. "Second grade recess?"

"Right before ours," Jazz said.

Milo felt a twinge of disappointment. So the diamonds he'd found in his desk had nothing to do with the jewel heist after all. Still . . . he and Jazz had solved their case!

"I don't understand," the woman said. "Why do you have my necklace?"

Milo handed it to her, then pointed at the girl. "Ask *her*."

"I didn't mean to steal it!" she wailed. "I was only borrowing it for the day."

"Ashley! *You* took my necklace?"

The girl turned her tear-stained face up to her mother. "Brianna gets to wear high-heeled sandals to school every day! Sparkly ones! I wanted to look fancy too."

Her mother's hands flew to her hips. "And you swore you had no idea where my necklace was!"

"I didn't," Ashley sobbed. "It felt bumpy on my neck, so I took it off and put it in my pocket during recess. I guess it fell out. I didn't know it was gone until I got back to class. I went to look right after school, but I couldn't find it."

Milo looked at Jazz. "Spencer."

She nodded.

The woman turned to them. "So you found my necklace on the playground?"

"Well . . . not exactly," Milo said. "Actually, I found it in my desk."

"Your *desk*?"

"The custodian put it in there," Jazz cut in. "She found it on the floor where Mandy dropped it."

The woman looked bewildered.

"Mandy?"

"A girl in our class," Milo explained. "See, Spencer has a crush on her—"

"Spencer? Who's Spencer?"

"He's the boy who found the diamond necklace on the playground," Milo said. "We figured it all out by working backward. Simple."

Jazz shot him a look.

"Okay, I may have slipped up once or twice along the way," Milo admitted. "But we got it in the end, right?"

The woman sank into a chair and rested her head in her hand.

"I'm sorry, Mom," her daughter said. "I wanted to tell you the truth. But I was scared the police would take me away." She started crying again.

"Ashley, don't be silly! That would never happen." Her mother got up and put her arms around her. "No wonder you haven't been feeling well. You're worried sick."

Ashley snuffled. "So I'm not in trouble?"

"You took my necklace without asking, and you lost it," her mother said. "Worst of all, you lied about it. Oh, yes. You're in trouble, all right. But with *me*, not the police."

Milo and Jazz exchanged a glance. Milo could tell they were thinking the same thing.

This would be a very good time to go back to class.

CHAPTER TEN

Milo hurried up the steps and rang the doorbell. He couldn't wait to show Jazz his new bug-collecting tool. Pretty soon he would know as much about bugs as Mr. Davenport!

When she answered, he held it up. "Ta-da!"

"What is that thing?" Jazz asked, stepping back to let him inside.

"A bug sucker."

"A *what*?"

"You use it to pick up little bugs without squishing them," he explained.

"See? You stick one tube over the bug and suck on the other tube, and the bug pops right into the jar. Mr. Davenport showed me how to make it. All you need is a jar and a couple of rubber tubes—"

Jazz's older brother Dylan looked up from his homework. "Davenport? Not *Dan* Davenport?"

"Well . . . yeah," Milo said. "I think so. He's my teacher."

"How do you know Mr. Davenport?" Jazz asked her brother.

"Are you kidding? Dynamite Dan? He's practically a legend," Dylan said. "Back when I was your age, he was the star of the high school basketball team. When he went up for a slam dunk, it was like he had rockets on his feet."

"Wow," Milo said.

Dylan sighed.
"He led the
team to state.
But then . . ."

"What?"
Jazz asked.

"It was the
last few seconds of
the game. The score was tied. Westview got
the ball and passed it straight to Dan. He
headed down the court."

"What happened?" Milo asked. "He
missed?"

"He never made the shot," Dylan said.
"Halfway down the court, Dynamite Dan
stopped in his tracks and let go of the ball."

"You're kidding!" Milo said.

Dylan shook his head. "Then he yelled 'Tiger!' and hit the floor."

"Tiger?" Jazz asked.

"Yeah! Everyone thought he'd gone loopy. Turned out he meant tiger *beetle*. It's this bug that's really hard to catch."

"So Westview lost the game because Mr. Davenport saw a bug?" Jazz asked.

"Naw. One of the other guys scooped up the ball and made the winning point," Dylan said. "But Coach had a total cow. He kicked Dan off the team."

"Poor Mr. Davenport," Milo said.

Dylan shrugged. "I don't think he minded all that much. Dynamite Dan liked basketball, but he was *really* into bugs."

"He's still into bugs," Milo said.

"Maybe he's still into basketball, too," Jazz said. "Remember that guy in the black van?"

Milo thought back. Dynamite Dan. Sunday night. "You mean—they were talking about a *basketball game?*"

"That's what I think." Jazz pulled out her purple notebook and pen. "I'm going to put it in our letter to Dash. Along with the big news about the real jewel heist."

"News?" Milo asked.

"Didn't you hear?"

He looked at his bug sucker. "I've been busy."

"They arrested the jewel thieves," Jazz told him. "It turned out to be an inside job. The jewelry store owner hired a gang of robbers to break into his store so he could collect the insurance."

"I don't believe it!" Milo said. "No wonder the robbers knew just what to do."

Jazz nodded. "The owner showed them where the cameras were, which jewelry was most expensive—everything."

"What did he do with the jewels?" Milo asked.

"The police found them hidden all over his house. Trixie Astor's necklace and tiara turned up at the bottom of the vegetable drawer."

Milo laughed. Then something in Jazz's open notebook caught his eye. Was that an ink splotch? No, it was crawling off the page. It was a bug!

He grabbed his bug sucker and leaned over the table. *Shwwwuuup*— Gulp.

"Did you get it? Where did it go?" Jazz peered into the jar, then looked up at him.

He stared back at her.

"Oh, Milo! You didn't *swallow* it!"

Milo nodded unhappily. "I don't know how it happened. I did just what

Mr. Davenport said. The jar, the rubber tubes, and . . . *oh*."

"What?" Jazz asked.

"I think he might also have said something about a small piece of nylon stocking for a screen," he admitted.

Jazz patted his arm. "You'll get it next time."

"I'm not sure I want to," Milo said. "I've kind of—well, I've kind of lost my *taste* for bug collecting."

Jazz laughed. "Well, you don't need to be a bug expert. You've already got the best hobby in the world."

"I do?" he asked.

"Absolutely, partner," she said. "Sleuthing!"

SUPER SLEUTHING STRATEGIES

A few days after Milo and Jazz wrote to Dash Marlowe, a letter arrived in the mail. . . .

Greetings, Milo and Jazz,

Your working-backward skills really sparkled on this case! I got a kick out of the jewelry store owner who hid the loot in his veggie drawer. He sounds almost as foolish as the culprit in The Case of the Forgetful Fullback. He hid a ruby in an 80,000-seat stadium—and then forgot which seat he'd hid it under! I can only say thank goodness for my jewel-sniffing dog. . . .

Happy Sleuthing!
—*Dash Marlowe*

Warm Up!
The best detectives (like myself) have quick, powerful minds. Keep yours in tip-top shape with these brain-stretching questions! (The answers are at the end of the letter.)

1. What has a foot on each side and one in the middle?
2. What is the next letter in this series: A E F H I K L M?
3. What goes up and down the stairs without moving?
4. A man rides into town on Friday. He stays three nights and leaves on Friday. How is this possible?

Fabulous Fakes: An Observation Puzzle

Not every jewel thief is a dullard! I received a frantic call from the owner of Glitz, a jewelry store. He told me his store had been robbed—a week ago!

Gary, the owner, hadn't noticed because the thief had taken several pieces of jewelry from the display—and had replaced each item with a similar but much cheaper piece! See if you're a better observer than Gary and try to spot the seven fakes!

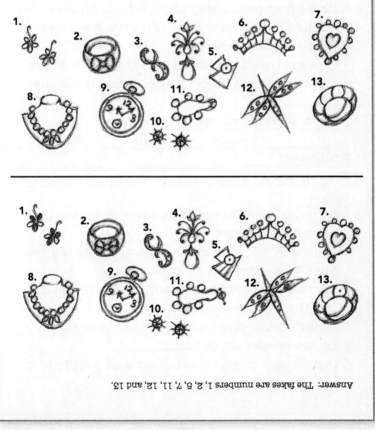

Answer: The fakes are numbers 1, 2, 5, 7, 11, 12, and 13.

Robbers in Love: A Logic Puzzle

Soon after ex-robbers Rocky, Louie, and Sal were released from prison, they all got serious crushes. What did each one do to impress his ladylove? And what did she do in return?

Look at the clues and fill in the answer box where you can. Then read the clues again to find the answer.

Answer Box (*see answers on next page*)

	Rocky	Louie	Sal
What he did			
What she did			

1. Sal did not give his crush his mug shot photo in a heart-shaped frame.
2. Louie introduced his crush to Number 8 on the Ten Most Wanted list.
3. Another guy showed his crush how fast he could pick the lock to her jewelry box.
4. Rocky's crush gave him a copy of *her* mug shot.
5. Louie's crush dumped him.
6. One robber's crush moved all her good jewelry to a safe deposit box.

The Case of the Not-Great Getaway: A Mini-Mystery

Check out this mystery—and draw a conclusion!

A while back I decided to get away from it all—no crime, no mystery for two weeks! I booked a room in a gorgeous hotel in Hawaii. But my hotel turned out to be the site of a jeweler's convention and the manager was worried about attempted robberies. I told him I was just there to relax!

I was lounging on my balcony with a cool glass of mango iced tea when I heard a knock on my door. As I walked across the room, the doorknob started to turn. I opened the door and saw a strange man. He said, "Oh, excuse me—I thought this was my room. Wrong floor, I guess." I watched him head for the elevator, then immediately called the hotel manager. "A thief was just on the 10th floor," I told him. "Call the police."

So how did I know what the man was up to?

Answer: The man wouldn't have knocked if he'd thought it was his room.

Answer to Logic Puzzle: Rocky gave his crush his mug shot photo in a heart-shaped frame, and she gave him her framed mug shot in return. Louie's crush dumped him after he introduced her to Number 8 on the Ten Most Wanted list. (She wasn't impressed, since she'd already dated Number 4.) Sal showed off by breaking into his crush's jewelry box. She was so impressed she moved all her good jewelry to a bank.

93

Loot: A Working Backward Puzzle

The DAILY CRISIS
THIEVES STEAL $90,000 FROM EASTHAM BANK

Working backward can even come in handy for criminals! I once planted a wire at the hideout of some thieves and here's what I heard.

Frank sounded angry. "That newspaper has got to be wrong," he said. "We got more than ninety thou from that bank!"

"How much *did* we get?" Al asked.

"Let's see," said Lucky. "We buried half the money in my backyard and split up the rest."

"I know I got $20,000," Al said.

Frank said, "Hmm. . . ."

And then there was silence.

The thieves couldn't figure it out.

Can you? How much money did they steal?

Was the newspaper right?

Answer: Frank was right and the newspaper was wrong. The robbers got $120,000. Not for long though, since my recording of their conversation got them arrested. (Here's how I figured out how much money they got:
Start with $20,000.
Multiply by 3, the number of robbers: 3 x $20,000 = $60,000.
Multiply by 2 for the half they buried: 2 x $60,000 = $120,000.)

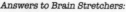

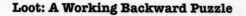

Answers to Brain Stretchers:
1. A yardstick
2. N. All these letters are made of straight lines; none are curved.
3. A rug
4. Friday is a horse.

Praise for . . .

"**The Milo & Jazz Mysteries** is a series that parents can enjoy reading with their children, together finding the clues and deducing 'whodunit'. The end of book puzzles are a real treat and will likely challenge most readers, regardless of age level."
—*Mysterious Reviews, Hidden Staircase Mysteries*

"Certain to be a popular series, **The Milo & Jazz Mysteries** are highly recommended additions to school and community library collections for young readers." —*Midwest Book Review*

★ **#1: The Case of the Stinky Socks**
"Gets it just right." —*Booklist*, starred review
Book Links' Best New Books for the Classroom

#2: The Case of the Poisoned Pig
Agatha Award nominee for best children's mystery
"Highly recommended." —*Midwest Book Review*

#3: The Case of the *Haunted* Haunted House
"Builds up to an exciting finish." —*Mysterious Reviews*

#4: The Case of the Amazing Zelda
"Fun page-turner." —*Library Media Connection*

#5: The Case of the July 4th Jinx
2011 Moonbeam Children's Book Awards
Silver Medal Winner

#6: The Case of the Missing Moose
#7: The Case of the Purple Pool

Collect these mysteries
and more—coming soon!

**Visit www.kanepress.com
to see all titles in
The Milo & Jazz Mysteries.**

ABOUT THE AUTHOR

Lewis B. Montgomery is the pen name of a writer whose favorite authors include CSL, EBW, and LMM. Those initials are a clue—but there's another clue, too. Can you figure out their names?

Besides writing the Milo & Jazz mysteries, LBM enjoys eating spicy Thai noodles and blueberry ice cream, riding a bike, and reading. Not all at the same time, of course. At least, not anymore. But that's another story. . . .

ABOUT THE ILLUSTRATOR

Amy Wummer has illustrated more than 50 children's books. She uses pencils, watercolors, and ink—but not the invisible kind.

Amy and her husband, who is also an artist, live in Pennsylvania . . . in a mysterious old house which has a secret hidden room in the basement!